RICHARD SCARRY'S
Great Big Schoolhouse
Readers

Snow Dance

Illustrated by Huck Scarry
Written by Erica Farber

STERLING CHILDREN'S BOOKS
New York

Huckle has a sled.
It is new. It is red.

Bump! Bump!
Oops! Do not sled
in here, Huckle!

3

Huckle goes up a hill.
Up! Up! Up!

He sleds down, down, down.

Bump! Bump! Oops!

A sled needs snow.

A sled needs snow to go!

Huckle goes to bed. He sleeps on the sled. Come on, snow, snow!

Huckle has a dream.

He dreams of snow.

Huckle wakes up. He has an idea.

Time to make snow!

Huckle gets ice.

Lowly gets a wagon.

Ella and Molly get ice.

Arthur and Skip get ice.

Wow! That is a lot of ice!

They take the ice.

They go to a hill.

They put the ice
on the hill.

Time to sled!

Huckle goes first.

His friends push.

The ice cracks. The sled tips.
They all fall. Oh, no!

They do a dance.

A dance for snow.

Step left! Step right!

Jump high!
Jump low!

Come on, snow, snow!

They jump. They spin. They all
fall down.

Come on, snow, snow!

Down comes one flake.

Down come some more.

See the snow, snow!

Time to sled. Zoom! Zoom!

Down the hill!

Thank you, snow dance!

Hooray for snow!

STERLING CHILDREN'S BOOKS
New York

An Imprint of Sterling Publishing
387 Park Avenue South
New York, NY 10016

ISBN 978-1-4027-9895-5 (hardcover)
ISBN 978-1-4027-9896-2 (paperback)

Produced by
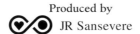 JR Sansevere

Distributed in Canada by Sterling Publishing
C/o Canadian Manda Group, 165 Dufferin Street
Toronto, Ontario, Canada M6K 3H6
Distributed in the United Kingdom by GMC Distribution Services
Castle Place, 166 High Street, Lewes, East Sussex, England BN7 1XU
Distributed in Australia by Capricorn Link (Australia) Pty. Ltd.
P.O. Box 704, Windsor, NSW 2756, Australia

For information about custom editions, special sales, premium and corporate purchases,
please contact Sterling Special Sales at 800-805-5489 or specialsales@sterlingpublishing.com.

Printed in China

Lot #:
2 4 6 8 10 9 7 5 3 1
11/13

www.sterlingpublishing.com/kids